7/4/14 ne

Peppa Pig

and the
Career Day

This book is based on the TV series *Peppa Pig*.
Peppa Pig is created by Neville Astley and Mark Baker.
Peppa Pig © Astley Baker Davies Ltd/Entertainment One UK Ltd 2003
www.peppapig.com

First edition 2018

Library of Congress Catalog Card Number pending
ISBN 978-1-5362-0344-8

18 19 20 21 22 23 APS 10 9 8 7 6 5 4 3 2 1

Printed in Humen, Dongguan, China

This book was typeset in Peppa.
The illustrations were created digitally.

Candlewick Entertainment
an imprint of Candlewick Press
99 Dover Street
Somerville, Massachusetts 02144

visit us at www.candlewick.com

3 9957 00206 3556

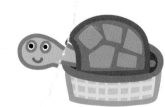

Peppa Pig and the Career Day

CANDLEWICK
ENTERTAINMENT

It's **Career Day** in Madame Gazelle's class.

There are some special visitors coming in to school today.

Peppa and her friends are very excited.

"You all know what I do," says Madame Gazelle.

"I'm your **teacher!**

It's my job to help you learn
to read, write, and do math.
And we learn art and music, too."

ABC
abcdefghijklm
nopqrstuvwxyz

12345

"I love **math**,"
says Suzy Sheep.

$$3 + 2 = 5$$

$$2 - 1 = 1$$

"**Reading** is my favorite,"
says Pedro Pony.

"Toot, toot!"

Everyone is happy to see Miss Rabbit, who is the

train engineer.

"I drive the train," she says.

"I take the grown-ups to work in the morning,
and then I bring them home at the end of the day!"

"Did you come to school today in the car or by bus?" asks Mr. Bull.

"Maybe you saw me digging up **the road!**
I have lots of vehicles and many tools."

Mrs. Cat is next.

"I work in an office," she says.

"My main tool is a **computer**."

"Hello!" says Mr. Zebra. "I come to all of your houses almost every day. I bring letters and packages.

I love being the **mail carrier.**"

"I remember the day you delivered my missing teddy bear!" says Peppa.

"That was a **special** delivery!"

Grandad Dog says, "I fix cars and trucks.
And I fill your gas tank when it's empty."

Miss Rabbit comes to the front of the room again.

"I also work at the **recycling center!**"

she says.

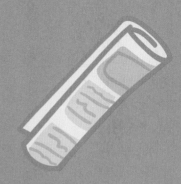

"Bottles go in the **green** boxes!"
says Peppa.

"And paper goes in the **red!**"
says Zoe Zebra.

Everyone knows Dr. Brown Bear.

"I try to help everyone stay healthy and **get better** when they don't feel well," he says. "I look down your throat with my tiny flashlight and give you medicine when you need it."

"Teeth are what I care about," says Dr. Elephant, the dentist. "Going to the dentist can be fun. Sometimes there are **stickers!**"

"Oooh," says Rebecca Rabbit. "I love stickers!"

"Ooooh," say the others. Everyone likes stickers.

Mrs. Zebra brings her potter's wheel to the front of the room.

"I'm an **artist**," she says.

"I make cups and bowls out of **clay** in my studio.
Being a potter is a really fun job!"

Miss Rabbit stands up again.

"Miss Rabbit!" says Suzy Sheep.
"Which job are you going to tell us about now?

Is it the one where you drive the
fire truck?"

"It is! When there's a fire,
I come to put it out."

Some jobs take people far from home.

That's where Captain Daddy Dog goes.

He is a **sea captain.**

He sails his boat all around
the world.

Mr. Fox is a **shopkeeper.**
He sells just about everything!

"Peppa and I have
a shop, too!"
says Suzy Sheep.

Miss Rabbit stands up again!

"Flying a **helicopter** isn't easy, but it's a job that I love.

I come to the **rescue** when no other vehicle can!"

"I make sure that boats don't hit the rocks when they come to shore. Do you know what I do?" asks Grampy Rabbit.

"Lighthouse keeper!"

shouts everyone.

"**I am a vet,**" says Dr. Hamster.
"I take care of pets and other animals."

Dr. Hamster has brought some of her
own pets to show the class.

Miss Rabbit hops up one more time.

"I like all of my jobs," she says.
"But one is my favorite.

The best job of all is selling ice cream."

Ice cream for everyone!